THE CHRONICLES OF DINAH LEE WRIGHT VOLUME 1

TALES OF AN OLD WEST SORCERESS

STEPHANNIE TALLENT

For more information, contact: stephannie@stephannietallent.com

First e-Book edition April 2021

Ebook ISBN: 978-1-942655-17-6
Print ISBN: 978-1-942655-18-3

www.stephannietallent.com

To Dave

What draws us into the desert is the search for something intimate in the remote.

— EDWARD ABBEY

CONTENTS

INTRODUCTION

Included herein are the tales of Dinah, a traveling sorceress in an alternate Old West, where magic is used by the bold, and both monsters and gods reside.

THE WITCH WATER

Salt crusted the caked, drying mud that surrounded the small brown pond. A sulfur stench burned Dinah's nose as the early afternoon sun beat down upon her bare neck, unprotected by hat or bandanna, as she crouched next to the pond, tips of her square-toed boots just shy of the murky water.

It was hot, hotter than normal in the Deseret Territory high plateaus, for what should be a mild late spring day. Stubby juniper trees and serviceberry bushes offered little shade. Her mule, Malyu, nibbled on a tuft of dry fescue grass near a juniper, tail swishing to keep away the flies attracted by the sweat on her dusty brown coat.

Sweat also ran from under Dinah's thick glossy black hair, bound up in a knot at the back of her neck, down her throat, then between her lean breasts, loose under a man's rough brown-dyed cotton shirt.

Dinah dipped a finger into the rancid pond, and tasted the tiniest drop of the sienna water. She gagged. Brackish and muddy and foul. Foul like something cursed died there, a black and hurtful death. She wiped her finger dry against her heavy canvas trousers.

She cussed softly. Jack Robertson wasn't going to be happy. His pretty roan shorthorn cattle weren't going to drink here, not without keeling over and feeding the turkey buzzards a couple hours later.

And this was the third watering spot ruined.

Dinah wasn't the sort to clean and bless the pond. Too many unjust skeletons dancing in her wake, even though she tried to be a good woman like she promised her mama, on her mama's deathbed.

That sort of magic, clean and pure and merciful, wouldn't come to her.

She could catch the bastard who did this, though, and make sure they did nothing like this again. Her magic, based on vengeance, tempered by justice, made her the best for catching evildoers, for folks not too proud to hire a foreign sorceress, the daughter of a Chinese prostitute and a bookish white man, an Art History professor from a fancy college back East.

You just don't foul water on purpose. It was too precious. And especially not water that kept alive the cattle and horses of the man she considered a second father. She could feel her righteous wrath bubbling up like a clear spring, clear like this pond should've been, fueling her magic.

She knew she'd need that strength.

WHEREAS DINAH POSSESSED A LEAN, whipcord strength in her small wiry frame, Mrs Genevieve Robertson was skinny to the point of illness, her huge blue eyes in her thin face the only chance of any prettiness. Those blue eyes held an ugly malice as she glanced disapprovingly at Dinah, caught mid-knock on the weathered gray doorframe of the sprawling Robertson ranch house.

Jack was like a father. Genevieve Robertson didn't have a drop of maternal affection for Dinah.

"I'm here for Jack," Dinah said, husky voice soft and polite.

"Mr Robertson," Mrs Robertson said, "is out back with his new filly." Sweat trickled down her gaunt, lined cheek, and a fly alit, but Mrs Robertson stood stock still, blocking the doorway, not raising a bony hand to wave away the fly until Dinah backed away from the door.

A cup of water would be a kindness, but Dinah knew she had no hope of any hospitality from Mrs Robertson, not if Jack wasn't present. That woman had dust in her veins, not a bit of warmth.

Dinah didn't know if it was because Dinah was half Chinese, dressed like a man, or both. Shoot, if she just knew Dinah's mama's history as a prostitute, that would be three big reasons for Mrs Robertson's animosity, a magic number sure to cement Mrs Robertson's hatred.

She walked around the ranch house to the corral back behind, kicking up dust with her boots, the glint of mica flakes glittering in the blistering sun.

A sturdy fence of raw branches nailed to sturdy pine posts encircled the soft dirt of the horse training corral. Dinah leaned up against the raw rails, resting her forearms across the top rail, long sleeves protecting against the rough sappy bark.

Two men also watched Jack work the filly. One was George Kinman, an old black cowboy who Dinah knew and liked. He treated people like he did horses, with a quiet respect and kindness, never mind the harm done to him before the War between the States, before he came west.

The other was a thin, pale man she'd not yet met. He had a nervous energy that Dinah wouldn't want around a young horse.

Then there was Jack Robertson, up on the back of a sorrel filly. The filly had a wide white blaze down her nose and socks up to her knees and hocks, all four legs. She sure was pretty, a copper penny dipped in cream, with the dished face and small compact body of an Arabian.

The filly bounced half-heartedly, dust swirling about her dainty hooves, but seemed fairly biddable, though tired, sweat streaking her coppery flanks and neck. Dinah figured Jack had been working with the filly at least a half hour, given how worn out both the filly and Jack looked.

Jack wore a battered, wide-brimmed straw hat, and a faded turkey red bandanna tucked around his neck, but his face was as sweat-streaked as the filly. He looked older than his fifty-five years, dark tanned skin lined, chestnut hair streaked with silver.

He looked tired. And worried.

He'd told Dinah that he'd come to Deseret to retire. That he'd earned a bit of rest.

Jack, trained as a surgeon, had taught at Columbia in New York up til a few years ago. He moved out to Deseret just three years ago, sick of university infighting and societal pressures, and bought his ranch in Cottonwood Valley.

The herd of shorthorn cattle came with the ranch. A skilled horseman, with plenty of family money, Jack decided to start a horse breeding program as well as running the cattle, bringing his prize black Morgan stallion Lincoln as the founding sire.

He was also a college friend and subsequent university colleague of her papa, and they'd corresponded over the years, after her papa had moved to Deseret. One of the first things Jack'd done after himself moving west was track Dinah down, pass on his condolences regarding her papa's death, and vow that he'd look out for his friend's daughter, given he and Mrs Robertson had none of their own.

Mrs Robertson was as unhappy about that as she was living in Deseret. Dinah didn't much care. Some people could never be happy. She didn't need Mrs Robertson's approval or respect, let alone affection.

"Meet Serafina," Jack called, wincing as he dismounted. The saddle the filly wore was a lightweight contraption, a little more to it than an Eastern saddle, but lacking the long- wearing heaviness of a typical Western saddle. He stroked the filly's face and blew into her nostrils gently. She didn't wear a bridle and bit, just a soft cotton hackamore.

"Isn't she lovely? Three and half years old and just the sweetest little lady."

"She sure is, Jack. But you know Malyu is my one true love," Dinah said. Dinah couldn't count the times she'd trusted her mule's sure feet and common sense to get her safely through treacherous terrain. "Can we find ourselves some shade, Jack? I need to tell you what I found."

Jack handed the filly off to the thin pale man, who took the reins gingerly. "Walk her then wipe her down, William," he said.

William complied, with a distinct lack of confidence that Dinah could pick out. Luckily the tired filly didn't notice, or just didn't care, and she didn't give more than one half- hearted skittish hop.

Jack headed back around to the front of the ranch house, Dinah at his heels, and led her into the simple parlor. He gestured to a faded green velvet stuffed chair, and Dinah sank into it. He plopped himself across from her on a delicate embroidered cream silk upholstered settee, not really made to hold his rangy six foot height.

Mrs Robertson silently entered the room, not even looking at Dinah, and placed a heavily laden tray in front of them. A teapot, a sugar bowl, a small carafe of milk, two delicate, rose-embellished china teacups on small plates, a plate full of scones, and two embroidered linen napkins. Dinah's mouth watered.

"Thank you, my love," he said to Mrs Roberston, smiling warmly. She smiled back, true love sweetening her features to prettiness.

"Help yourself, my dear," he said to Dinah.

Dinah wouldn't have trusted anything that Mrs Robertson served her, but figured Mrs Robertson wasn't going to poison her husband, not with that gaze they exchanged. She poured herself a cup of tea, adding a little slop of milk, and picked up a scone as well. She nibbled at the edge. Lemon, with a tart brightness that pleased her. She put the scone down on the delicate china plate, nestled next to her tea cup.

"The pond up on the ridge is fouled," Dinah said, husky voice soft. "Not by natural means. Just like the other two ponds. Who doesn't like you, Jack?"

Jack ate a scone in two bites and washed it down with unsweetened black tea. "Here? I don't know," he said. "Back east, I have enemies. None here that I know of."

"I can track whoever did this," Dinah said. Unspoken was *and get rid of them*. "But I can't purify the ponds. Will the cattle be okay?"

"If the spring up valley stays clean, and if the snow melt suffices to keep the creek flowing." He cleared his throat. "Dinah, do you know of anyone who *can* purify the water?"

She took a larger bite of her scone, chewed, considered. "I know someone I can ask," she said. "I can't promise they will, though." Jack's reputation for hiring and harboring an eclectic mix of ranch hands and fair dealing would definitely help.

But he was still a white man, living on what used to be someone else's land.

A DAY later she was back up on the plateau, kneeling next to the pond in the midday heat. The stench stung her nose and brought tears to her eyes as she'd ridden up.

A dead jackalope bobbed in the water near the center of the pond, a bit of slimy pond weed trailing off one of its little antlers.

A scrub jay cried to her in concern as she dipped a finger into the pond. *Don't touch, don't touch*, he screeched, flying out from his perch on a nearby juniper, circling around her head three times, and back to his tree.

Scrying wasn't easy for her, but she knew it was the best place to start, given she'd not found any natural, non- magical traces to track. Whoever doing this was sneaky but smart.

She was sneakier and smarter. Had to be.

She sat back and unsheathed her small eating knife, kept safe hanging on her belt. Gritting her teeth, she cut across the ball of her left thumb, deep enough for a smooth upwelling of blood. She let it drip into the still muddy water, hand held a couple feet above the pond, red circular ripples pushing out with each drop.

Seven drops should do it.

Something unseen in the water pulled, leeching at her strength and will, dragging her hand down towards the pond like her suddenly streaming blood was a rope it'd caught hold of.

Spots swam before her eyes, like riding into the sun too long.

Strong teeth that smelled of sweet hay gripped the back of her shirt collar, catching a hank of her hair, and yanked her back just before she fell into the pond.

She landed full out sprawled on her back, gazing up into Malyu's deep brown eyes. The mule gently wuffed her face, soft lips nibbling on Dinah's nose.

Dinah wished she could just lay there, momentarily safe from the evil spirit in the pond, but she had to look. She had to know.

She kept her still-bleeding hand behind her, as far from the pond as possible.

The dead jackalope was gone. She didn't know if the pond ate it, or it just sank, water logged fur finally dragging it down. The surface was still, reflecting the noonday sun and high cirrus clouds, all colored with a pinkish tinge from her blood.

Maybe she could still see something...*there*. A tiny wisp of a figure, a face, too indistinct and blurred to identify. Masculine? she thought, but thin and sickly and skittish. A feel of desperation and the willingness to do anything, hurt anything and anyone, to achieve his truest desires.

What were those desires? She grasped for any bit of motivation, even physically reached with her bleeding hand towards the pond. Behind...a second figure? A bubble rose to the pond surface and popped, belching sulfurous gas, and oily ripples erased the faint figures.

Dinah slumped back.

Malyu nibbled the tips of her hair, her version of a gentle hand on Dinah's shoulder. Dinah stroked her velvety soft nose, leaning her cheek against her warm fuzzy face, her breath mingling with Malyu's sweet grassy exhalations.

Dinah had no clue where to look next.

The scrub jay squawked again, then winged over to her, landing on the horn of Malyu's saddle, small dark eyes meeting hers. *Intruder. New.* He flew back to his juniper.

Well. She wrapped her hand with a clean bandanna, then mounted Malyu and headed down the trail to the ranch house.

WHAT'S new to a flighty scrub jay? Anyone who showed up to that pond for the first time could be new. New to the Deseret Territories? New to Cottonwood Valley? New to their sorcerous power?

Dinah hadn't decided for sure what that jay meant, but she figured she could start by talking to Jack's new ranch hand, the skinny nervous fellow William. She arranged to meet him in Mrs Robertson's parlour that evening after supper.

"I don't know anything about the water," he said, pale eyes not meeting hers, right eyelid twitching. He perched on the edge of the cream settee like he was afraid it was going to swallow him up whole.

She wanted to smack him, stop that twitching.

Mama had said her temper could get her into trouble. "Surely you're not accusing my cousin," Mrs Robertson said, entering the parlour, bearing the same tray as before, same tea cups, even a small selection of scones and cookies.

Well, that explained his pinched nervous look. Must be a family thing.

"Not at all, Mrs Robertson," said Dinah. "Just hoping to get a different perspective."

Neither William nor Mrs Robertson appeared mollified.

"Have some tea, Dinah, and a scone. I saw how you liked the lemon one the other day. You hardly ate a thing at supper." She poured a cup of tea, added a dollop of cream, and passed it to Dinah, followed by a small scone, glossy with a sugar glaze. Mrs Robertson set the tray down on the small spindle-legged table between the settee and Dinah's velvet chair.

Dinah took a sip of tea, a nibble of the scone. Something tasted a little off. It lacked the fresh brightness of the scone the day before. She took another bite.

The sugar glaze. It tasted foul, now, foul as the hungry tainted pond.

Dinah tried to spit it out, fingers spasming on the horsehair stuffed arms of the velvet chair, her clouding vision getting just a glimpse of Mrs Robertson's satisfied face, of William's smug smile, as she toppled forward.

Blackness.

~

Dream World. The sun warmer and brighter, the sky bluer, the sweet smell of sage and creosote stronger.

Morning, based on the angle of the sun, not early evening.

Dinah sat cross-legged in dappled sunlight, on a large flat sandstone boulder in a small clearing on the valley floor, surrounded by cottonwoods. A small bubbling spring that gave birth to a small creek, clear water cascading across polished rocks, was below her perch.

She wore a simple white cotton shift, long enough to reach past her knees. Her unbound hair streamed down her back, a glossy black waterfall of hair, a soft sage breeze teasing the ends. Her long narrow feet were bare. She reached to her neck, to the charm she always wore on a leather lace. Gone.

No weapons. No charms. And she was tired, so tired. She sighed and looked up.

Canine-headed, human-bodied Coyote lazed on a similar sandstone boulder across from her, holding a cigarillo in one tanned human hand, bringing up to his toothy snout once in a while to take a puff. He was fully clothed: thick faded black cotton trousers, finely tooled black leather boots with turquoise leather insets, a black wool vest with silver buttons over a white shirt. His black wool cowboy hat, pushing his big coyote ears down to either side, featured a black leather band studded with Sleeping Beauty turquoise nuggets.

And three knives she could readily see, two for throwing and one, a jagged tip Bowie, for gutting prey. Or enemies.

"Howdy, darlin'," he said. "What sort of trouble did you get yourself into now?"

"Leaping without looking," she said. "Underestimating someone. The usual."

"I dunno. You always seem to keep your head about you." He yipped, tongue lolling, twitching those big ears of his, gesturing at his coyote head in case she didn't get his point.

She waited patiently til he stopped his yodeling. "Any advice? I need to get back, pronto." Never hurt to ask, as long as she took what he said with a very measured grain of salt.

"Didn't you maybe think you're right where you need to be, darlin'?" He touched the brim of his hat, smiled, then vanished. Just gone.

She hated that. He always did that, flat out disappearing after saying something more than a bit cryptic. And by the time she saw him again, she wouldn't need his clarification. 'Course, that's probably why he did it.

Enough nattering.

She slipped off the sandstone, the roughness of the boulder pulling up her shift to past mid thigh. She yanked the shift back down once she got her feet on the ground, stumbling a little, damp sand scrunching up between her toes.

She thought she heard a soft sigh of disappointment. "Just git if you're not going to give me any more guidance," she called.

A soft yip in reply, then silence. *So. In the right place.*

Mrs Robertson and cousin William did not seem the sorts to traverse the Dream World.

Or at least, not this Dream World. She thought back to the packed streets of Boston, the crowds, when she'd visited that city after her parents had died, trying to find a place with her papa's people. Maybe their Dream World was like that, carriages and trains and ships and people and noise, so much noise.

Give her the high desert and fertile river carved valleys of Deseret, which this Dream World mirrored.

So, despite the deed of poisoning her, despite the taste of the poison, so like the sickened pond water, maybe they weren't responsible for the water fouling?

She reached out her hands, palms up, beseeching.

"Please, may I have boots? Or moccasins?"

She put the tiniest kiss of power behind her words. Not a threat, an offering.

Soft doeskin enveloped her feet. Moccasins, ankle-high, held closed with a tooled silver button with an inset turquoise stone.

"Thank you." She didn't know if there was any distinct entity here, beyond the Dream World having a somnolent sentience itself, but saying thank you was just good manners.

She kneeled by the spring and drank deeply. The water was sweet and pure, a little bit milky on her tongue. She felt stronger, more awake. She drank more, so much her belly felt overfull. She hoped it was helping her real world body. Not much else she could do otherwise.

Then she headed downstream, carefully picking her way amongst the tumbled sandstone boulders and cottonwood roots.

TIME FLOWS STRANGELY in the Dream World. Dinah felt like she'd been traveling for hours to reach the widening of the valley, the location echoing that of Jack's homestead. This valley was empty of any human touch. Yellow and purple wildflowers attracted fat buzzing bees and swooping butter- flies. Dense sweet grass carpeted the valley floor. Paradise for Jack's shorthorn cattle and his herd of Morgans and Arabs, if those creatures could visit the Dream World.

The creek too had widened, joined by other small tributaries, to a shallow, slow-moving river, teaming with leaping iridescent rainbow trout, water-skating stick bugs, and chatty gray and yellow flycatchers swooping around catching said bugs.

A scrub jay winged around her head, then perched on her hand when she held out her arm. It studied her, its dark eyes bright with intelligence. It was surprisingly heavy, a bit larger and just more there than its real world counterpart.

Greetings. It bobbed its bright blue head.

Dinah liked jays and their cousins, crows and ravens. They didn't know when to shut up, but they had good hearted, curious, intelligent natures. She treated them with kindness and respect, and they reciprocated.

More trustworthy than humans that way.

Good hunting, cousin, she responded.

Seek intruder? it asked, cocking its head sideways.

He is here?

The jay nodded. *Follow.*

~

THE JAY FLEW SLOWLY, accommodating Dinah's long-legged lope, til it reached a spot where a small islet rising out of the water temporarily split the river. The jay squawked and flew away.

Upon that islet was a flat sandstone, about six feet across, pretty much filling the entire islet. Its gritty golden surface reflected the sunlight.

And upon that, lay a male form, dressed in heavy blue canvas trousers, a stained white button-front shirt with the sleeves rucked up to his elbows, and a straw cowboy hat, sleeping deeply. Black miasma trickled from his limp hand to the river, dripping into the clear water and turning it a dark murky color downstream.

Jack.

"No," she breathed, and the figure stirred.

"Dinah?" he said drowsily, sitting up, tugging at his sleeves.

She nodded. Couldn't speak. Betrayal thickened her tongue.

"Whatever are you doing here, and dressed like that?" His eyes sharpened as he took in her cotton shift and doeskin moccasins. "Where am I?"

"The Dream World. The Deseret that should be, if folk like you weren't there to ruin it." She couldn't help the bitterness. Wasn't *her* that betrayed *him*.

"Ruin it? I don't want to ruin it. I love my horses, my cattle, my land." Even as he spoke, that darkness dripped faster, carving a channel in the sandstone, poisoning the river, and subsequently, poisoning the water sources in the real world.

Murdering his land.

Murdering *the* land.

Jack's name might be on the deed, but that land belonged to everyone. The scrub jays, the jackalopes, the mule deer. The coyotes, the horny toads, the thunderbirds.

"But you are, Jack, you are. And why?"

"I love my wife," he said slowly. "Genevieve isn't happy here."

"And you'll destroy the land to give you the excuse to leave?" *Because you aren't man enough to admit to yourself what you want?* Times like now she wanted a lightning strike from the clear blue sky to spark a purifying wildfire, destroying every white man who tried to take control of this land.

Just a prayer and an offering to a thunderbird ....

But she wouldn't do that. Not cause that much devastation.

But summon a thunderbird to destroy just him and Genevieve and William...that had some appeal, might assuage her fury.

But no. Much as she wanted to right now. Thunderbirds didn't deserve to have that destruction hanging over them, anyways. Bright beings of fire and lightning, purer in spirit than she was.

If only she herself could pull lightning out of the sky...but as angry as she was, she didn't want Jack's blood on her hands. He was still like a second father to her. One she hated right now, but still, kin.

Kin of her now broken heart.

He shrank back from her, keeping the few feet of river between them.

She never could keep her face blank. She always lost at poker, too. She could only imagine how she appeared in the dreamlands.

"Fierce and bright, vengeance on two feet," Coyote offered from behind her. "I wouldn't want to be facing you."

She glanced back him. Still coyote-headed, his amber eyes cold. He held out his big knife, the jagged-tip Bowie, hilt first, balancing the blade on his fingertips, and jerked his chin towards Jack.

"Blood can cleanse," Coyote said, his voice iron hard, stepping up beside her, still offering the knife.

Just like that, her fury was doused. Her cotton shift wasn't enough to keep chills from enveloping her, even in the bright spring sunlight.

"That can't be the only way," she said.

Jack was standing up on the sandstone, staring at the darkness flowing from both hands, pitting the stone, muddying the water. "This is me? It's my fault?"

He looked to Coyote. "I am so sorry. I'm not doing this on purpose, but it's my responsibility."

Jack waded through the few feet of river separating them and took the Bowie knife from Coyote.

"Find someone to love the ranch," he said to Dinah. "Help Genevieve sell the cattle and horses."

"Blast you to the seven hells," Dinah said. "I won't let you do this."

Jack ignored her, looking to Coyote. "What do I do?"

Coyote shrugged, amber eyes glinting. "What you feel you need to."

Jack nodded, then pushed up his left sleeve and sliced at his wrist. Blood spurted, then flowed, mingling with the blackness that had already joined the river.

No more blackness poured from his hands. Just blood from his wound.

The blood streamed so fast from his wrist that Dinah thought Jack should already be drained. As it was, Jack teetered, then crumpled to his knees, still holding his arm out over the river.

Coyote gripped her shoulder, keeping her from going to Jack. "Wait," he hissed.

The river water downstream started to glow, iridescent sparks jumping off its surface like the rainbow trout earlier, clearing the murkiness, racing down the river to the limits of the poison.

"Enough," Coyote said, reaching out to Jack and grasping his wounded wrist. Jack cried out, but the bleeding stopped, the wound knitting closed.

Jack had aged. Old, so old, a decade or two older than his fifty five, his face deeply lined, his eyes milky, his hair a shock of white against his tanned leathery skin. He looked like a dying barrel cactus, all wizened and fibrous, falling in on itself.

"Wake up," Coyote said. "Talk to your wife, get this settled. Wake up." He paused, then added, "And if you come here again, causing harm, I'll gut you myself." He smiled viciously. "Remember that. Wake up."

Three time's a charm. Jack disappeared.

"I could've helped," Dinah whispered. "I thought he was going to die."

"Well, he will, sooner than he otherwise would've." Coyote stretched, lean muscled arms to the sky, shedding his clothes with the breeze and a quick wink at Dinah. He then plopped on the ground, all coyote, no human. *Wake up, wake up, wake up,* he yipped.

And she did.

~

DINAH GAGGED, then spat up the bits of scone she'd eaten. She was back in the parlour, no time having passed at all. Shock replaced Genevieve and William's smugness as she stood up.

"You knew," Dinah said. "You knew it was Jack. And you didn't tell him."

Genevieve shook her head. "I didn't know for sure. I was just hoping with you out of the picture, he'd give up and we could go home."

"Well, you better go see to him. He's sore wounded. He healed the water, at great cost to himself."

Genevieve blanched and ran from the parlour. Her anguished wail cut the quiet evening air, shaking loose dust and spiders from the high beams of the ceiling. Dinah guessed that Jack looked like he did in the Dream World, a broken wizened version of himself. Shock to anyone, let alone his wife who let him destroy the world for her personal happiness.

"You might as well go to her, too, cousin William," said Dinah. "Maybe help them settle their affairs here."

She left the parlour to go pack up Malyu. She didn't even want to spend the night at the Robertson homestead, not one more moment under that roof.

Maybe someday she would forgive Jack. Not tonight, not tomorrow, though.

~

THE STABLE, a large barn-like building of fresh unpainted pine boards and a peaked roof with storage for hay in the loft area, had ten fully contained stalls either side of a central packed dirt galley way, each stall padded with fresh straw bedding. Malyu had been housed in one of the larger corner stalls, big and comfortable enough that she stayed in it, rather than opening the latch as she'd been known to do.

Serafina had a middle stall; Lincoln, the black Morgan stallion, was in the corner stall kittycorner to Malyu's. It was obviously his, built with extra boards to strengthen the walls. Dinah patted his nose as she walked by his stall. He seemed like a good tempered stallion, but he *was* a stallion. A few other horses that Dinah didn't recognize occupied the other stalls.

The whole place smelled of fresh hay and straw and horse. Refreshing, after the still thick air of the parlour.

Coyote was waiting for her in Malyu's stall in the stable, chewing on a handful of sweet feed, molasses and oats. He swiped some oats out of his cupped palm with that long pink tongue of his, then held his hand out to Malyu to nibble at the feed with her sensitive whiskery lips.

Malyu was already all packed up, thick wool blanket cushioning her simple saddle, packed saddlebags tied down behind it, a saddle britchen strapped around her rump and a collar around her chest.

"Ready to go, darlin'?" asked Coyote.

"That I am."

"Think he'd miss that fine filly?"

"I think if he just loses Serafina, he gets off easy," Dinah said, taking Malyu's reins and leading her out. Behind her she could hear Coyote coaxing Serafina out of her stall and tacking her up.

"Let's go, Malyu," Dinah said, turning her mule to the moonlit, mica dusted trail, accompanied by the gentle *hoo hoo* of an owl and the creaking trill of a goatsucker.

Even if she lost the kin of her heart, she kept the land of her soul safe.

CHRISTMAS EVE AT THE JACKALOPE SALOON

This story is a mash up of two of my series: Dinah's Weird West, and Laila's alternative, contemporary Los Angeles.

Laila only has a cameo, but her Pekingese puppy Daiyu is the other major character in this story.

Even in the dusty battered cowtown of Jackalope Springs in Deseret, folks celebrated the birth of the Christian savior.

Dinah eyed the cheap red and silver colored lead tinsel hanging off the rafters in between the taxidermy rabbits, antelope heads, and jackalopes (some of which Dinah reckoned to be real, not just stitched together fakes).

The Jackalope Saloon proprietor, Mr Reginald Smith, had sprung for a spell to keep that tinsel glittering, even high up in the rafters, away from the newly-installed gas chandeliers. Errant flashes of light from the tinsel were zapping the card players at the rickety tables that filled the room in the eyes, to their great annoyance.

Dinah wasn't a believer, but she admitted the glittering tinsel was pretty in a cheap way. 'Specially if it annoyed the card sharps.

Freshly cut juniper and pine boughs were carefully tucked

between the rafters and between the spindles and handrail of the staircase going up to the second floor at the back of the saloon. Their thick piney scent glossed over the sticky smells of spilt liquor and old blood.

Dinah tossed down her drink, a mix of lukewarm, watered-down whiskey and apple cider, tasting weak alcoholic heat and little else.

Watered down. She didn't know if she should feel insulted that Frank back there behind the bar was trying to cheat a half Chinese daughter of a prostitute and a fancy over-educated East Coast white man, both long since deceased, or trying to cheat a bounty huntin' sorceress who passed as a teenage boy most of the time.

Neither spoke well of his character, in her opinion. Or intelligence.

Maybe he was just an equal opportunity cheat.

Didn't really matter. She'd just gotten to this town a day ago, to rest after a job, and would be moving on in just a few. The more reputable folks in town were spending Christmas Eve in the small All Souls chapel down the dusty street, listening to the fiery preaching of Reverend James B. Edwards. Dinah didn't fancy herself a Christian, and couldn't stomach the natterings of a brimstone preacher who tended to think anyone the same color as her was a hell fated animal, but she wanted a bit more company than he own, this evening.

She loved her mule Malyu, but frankly, cuddling up to nine hundred pounds of pungent horseflesh for a second night didn't interest her, as warm and quiet as the stable was and as much as Malyu liked her soft nose scritched just so.

So the saloon it was. Maybe she could play a hand or two of cards. Or just drink herself silly on cheap whiskey cocktails.

There were the good time gals upstairs ... but that didn't really interest her either.

For the first time, Dinah was surprised to realize she'd let her guard down enough to actually be lonely. She'd thought she'd conquered that weakness.

Her thought winged across the half-filled saloon, out the half-opened wooden door, and into the starry velvet sky, kissed by winter storm clouds: *I do wish I wasn't so alone right now.*

DAIYU CURLED up on the green velvet couch, her fuzzy chin resting on her black furry paws. She gave a mournful little howl as the front door of the carriage house shut on the heels of her mistress, Laila, and Laila's Djinn companion, Oz.

They were off to Laila's mother's family in Azusa, north- east of Los Angeles, for a Christmas gathering.

Laila's Tia Margarita was deathly allergic to dogs, so that meant Daiyu, Laila's *very* hairy Pekingese puppy, had to stay home on Christmas Eve.

All Laila had talked about today was Tia Elena's tamales (green and red, pork and beef, cheese and corn, and various permutations of all those ingredients) and Tio Pablo's rum- spiked Mexican hot chocolate, sweet and spicy with cinnamon and a hint of ancho chili, til Daiyu couldn't help but drool all over herself.

Then Laila left Daiyu behind. She brought Oz: Oz! who as far as Daiyu was concerned was an untrustworthy evil demon requiring Daiyu's constant surveillance to keep him honest and harmless.

But left Daiyu behind. Alone.

Yes, Laila had left the TV on for her, tuned to her favorite channel (HGTV; Daiyu had a huge puppy crush on the Property Brothers, and if she wasn't Laila's sworn Lion Dog protector, she'd have found her way to Jonathan).

And Laila had fed her a special dinner of chicken breast and sweet potatoes and chicken-broth flavored brown rice.

Afterwards, she'd even given her a special teeth-cleaning, peanut butter flavored chewy, but ...

... she'd left Daiyu *behind*.

Daiyu had never, in all her short eight months of life, ever been left completely alone.

She was bewildered and sad and so, so lonely.

She threw back her head and howled once more. *I wish I wasn't so alone right now.*

~

DINAH DIDN'T KNOW who was more surprised: Frank, in the midst of another pour of watered whiskey and cider into Dinah's glass; Dinah, patiently waiting because she simply didn't have anything better to do; or the fluffy black Pekingese puppy that popped out of the air right in front of Dinah on the whiskey-sticky, stained bar top.

Frank screeched and splashed whiskey all over his grimy cotton shirt and black wool vest, Dinah jumped despite herself, and the puppy started barking, surprisingly deep barks for all of its five or so pounds.

"Hush, hush," Dinah said, reaching forward to pet its little round head.

Her mama had told her stories about Lion Dogs, fierce loyal protectors, and their worldly appearance as royal Pekingese dogs. The power pulsing from the tiny body in front of her impressed her, and Dinah was admittedly very difficult to impress.

On top of that power, the puppy had the softest jet black fur, and the deepest brown eyes.

Dinah was just a little bit in love, just like that.

She'd never met man or woman who stirred that emotion in her, platonic or not. But this little bit of fur and bone and fierceness ... she buried in face in the dog's fur, smelling the sweet fragrances of cinnamon and ginger.

~

DAIYU, for her part, was totally smitten as well. This woman in front of her, with her glossy straight black hair and fine features, reminded Daiyu of her first human, Mrs Wu, who had subsequently sworn her to Laila's service.

Mrs Wu had been strict but fair, and Daiyu could sense those characteristics in the young woman in front of her. And the hint of sorcerous power, firmly held in check and exquisitely mastered, excited Daiyu. She adore her Laila, but Laila, as clever as she was, had only human wit and ingenuity.

This woman, with her lightning-sparking amber eyes, smelled of rich magical potential. Daiyu was impressed.

Daiyu murfled in the woman's sleek hair, smelling pine and campfire smoke, even as the woman did the same to her. She licked the woman's cheek with her tiny pink tongue before the woman slowly sat back.

"I'm Dinah," the woman said.

Daiyu, she thought back, as hard as she could. *Black Jade*.

Dinah's brow wrinkled. "Jade?" she said.

Close enough! Daiyu yapped in excitement, then leaped off the bar into Dinah's hastily opened arms.

"Hungry, little Jade?" Daiyu licked Dinah's chin.

"Frank, if that room upstairs is still available for rent tonight, I would like it for this little creature and myself. Send up some of that roast beef I heard Mrs Townsend had cooked up next door at the boarding house. And if you have bottle of your better whiskey with the cork still waxed, send that on up as well."

Frank opened his mouth, ready to argue. The stench of rotting teeth hit Daiyu, and she snuggled closer to Dinah, breathing in her campfire scent.

"Don't even tell me dogs aren't allowed," Dinah said. "I've seen rats in here twice the size of this little dog."

DINAH CARRIED Daiyu up the stairs to the second floor and down the hallway, ignoring the soft gasps and moans from behind closed doors.

Lit gas sconces flickered along the hallway walls, the faint smell of rotten garlic from the acetylene gas tainting the air. Dinah wondered about the condition of the gas pipes in the saloon, newly installed though they were. She'd have to mention it to Mr Smith tomorrow, even if it was Christmas.

The door to the last room on the right was ajar, and Dinah nudged it open with one booted foot. The room itself was small, most of it filled by an iron bed with a couple gray, moth eaten woolen blankets and a lumpy stuffed mattress. A gas sconce on the wall near the door put out a little bit of light when Dinah turned it on, opening the gas flow and directing a spark from her fingertip at the mantle, lighting it. The light burned cleanly in the room, at least. No rotten garlic smell. No leaks here.

The small light from the sconce was put to shame by the brilliant light of the full moon, streaming through the sheer- curtained window on the opposite side of the room.

Daiyu could smell a bit of rosewater and sweat, left over from the last occupant of the room. She wriggled, and Dinah set her down on the bare wooden floor. Daiyu dashed about: under the bed and back out (no rats here), then to the window, bouncing up and down, trying to look out but having no luck getting enough height.

Dinah scooped her up and placed her on the bed. "Good enough, Jade?" she asked Daiyu, sitting next to her and pulling off her boots. Thick woolen socks encased her narrow feet. Daiyu could see where Dinah had darned them, multiple times, and another spot on the heel of the left foot that was going to need mending soon too.

Daiyu loved chewing on Laila's merino wool hiking socks, which Dinah's socks resembled. Laila had lots of socks, so many they filled a dresser drawer.

She didn't think Dinah had very many socks. She would not chew on Dinah's socks.

Dinah leaned back, arranging a thin pillow behind her against the iron rails at the head of the bed. She sighed, stretching from her toes to her fingertips, then patted the spot right next to her. Daiyu scampered there, turned once, and lay down, snugged up to Dinah, with her head on the pillow. She glanced up at Dinah. Dinah just stroked Daiyu's little head.

Seemed like the pillow was fair game. Daiyu closed her eyes in puppy bliss.

ABOUT A HALF HOUR later a knock announced the arrival of dinner. By that time, the moonlight from the window had dimmed, thick winter storm clouds scudding across its face. It would snow soon, Dinah bet. She could feel it in her bones.

She fed the puppy bits of rare roast beef, Jade taking them daintily from her fingertips, not spilling any of the succulent juices on herself or on the bed. A perfect little lady.

They'd just finished eating the beef and potatoes when something banged against the window, knocking it fully open.

Frigid winter air blasted snow flurries into the room.

A large white owl with bloody pink eyes flew in on softly beating wings, lithely avoiding getting tangled in the curtains that the wind was whipping around.

The owl's massive talons, cruelly hooked and gleaming in the gas lamp as if dipped in fresh blood, were aimed directly at Jade.

Dinah leapt up and fumbled for the protective charm at her neck, taken from a fox sorcerer's stash of magic last fall, but the leather thong was hopelessly tangled in her hair, and the charm out of reach.

But she didn't need it.

Little Jade faced the owl, her canines thickening and lengthening even as Dinah desperately yanked at the charm.

The little puppy was shape changing into one of the lion dogs of legend.

She wasn't quite full grown: Dinah pictured the lion dogs as massive, grizzly bear-sized beasts, and this one was more the size of a hefty puma. A fierce growl, ever deepening, culminated in a powerful roar that rattled the window frame and whipped the snow-heavy curtains about.

The owl was no match for a lion dog, even just half grown, and it knew it. The owl swiftly spun away, not even trying to finish its stooping attack, and flew out the window on snow laden wings.

Or maybe, it was only there to gather information.

The leather thong untangled just like that. Dinah pulled it off, then wrapped the cord around her wrist. She supposed her shirt sleeve could magically grown longer and prevent her access to the charm, but she doubted it.

"Well, little Jade," Dinah said, carefully shutting the window and locking the latch. "That sure was an interesting visitation." Owls meant death, and a *white* owl doubly so: Dinah didn't think this was the end of the night's troubles.

The pup, back to her normal tiny fluffy self, barked up at her in agreement.

~

DINAH SNAPPED AWAKE. Jade, deep in a doggy dream, feet softly paddling, was a warm lump against her side.

Dinah wasn't sure what had woke her, but paramount was the fact that she hadn't intended on sleeping in the first place.

Yet she had fallen asleep.

That just wasn't natural. At least, not for her.

A white mist was sneaking between the edges of the window and the frame. She squinted at it; the moon had nearly set, and just a bit of light reflected from the heavily snow covered street and roofs.

The mist coalesced into a slender figure.

A woman, dressed in a sheer white gown that glittered like icicles. That gown did nothing to provide modesty, outlining her lithe figure the way it did. Long white hair, dancing like a living creature in the cold wind, and pale silver eyes that gleamed with avarice. The woman's pale features were delicate, nearly brittle. Her full lips, the only lush thing about her, were a rosy tint of lilac. She smelled of ice, long frozen in the depths of caverns, never exposed to sunlight.

She was beautiful and terrifying all at the same time. Jade still slumbered, twitching a little, softly squeaking. The woman smiled.

"Adorable, isn't she?" she asked Dinah. "And so much power, in such as tiny body."

The charm at Dinah's wrist would do nothing to protect her against one such as this. And it didn't look like Jade could do anything, trapped in her dreams.

"You can call me Yuki, little cousin from across the sea," the woman said. "I'm just here for the dog. Give her to me, and I'll leave you alone."

The dog? No way in all the frozen hells was Dinah going to hand over sweet little Jade to this creature. The pup didn't deserve to be a slave, and Dinah knew that was what she'd be. Never mind giving handing someone as powerful as Jade to a snow demoness.

Dinah swept her gaze along the woman's body, then brazenly met her eyes. "Maybe I don't want to be left alone," she said.

The woman laughed. "Two lonely souls for the price of one," she said. "You intrigue me, my girl."

"Let me turn on the light," Dinah said, bolder now. "Let me see you better."

The woman gestured in acquiescence, an amused smile twisting those full lips.

Dinah stood up and turned her back on the woman, one of the bravest things she thought she'd ever done.

She fiddled with the light switch, giving the lamp a good tug at the same time, taking care to hide her movements. She heard a snap within the wall and felt the lamp loosen.

She smelled rotten garlic, seeping through the join of the lamp to the wall.

She turned on the gas.

"I'm just going to light this now," she said over her shoulder. "Just a little touch of magic."

"Go ahead, my girl," the woman said, stepping up right behind Dinah, one cold hand caressing the back of Dinah's neck.

Dinah directed sparks not just at the mantle, but at the spot where the lamp was affixed to the wall.

She dove onto the bed, covering Jade with her body and yanking the wool blankets over the both of them.

The lamp's mantle did indeed ignite.

So did the jet of gas from the broken pipe, right into the face of the woman.

The woman shrieked, the sound of a winter storm forcing its way through a barricaded door, a wail that pierced Dinah's ears cruelly and even awakened little Jade from her sorcerous slumber. Jade howled, but not loud enough to cover that creature's screeches.

That shriek petered out after a few minutes. Dinah cautiously poked her head out from under the covers.

A large puddle soaked the wooden floor just under the sconce. Dinah relaxed, then flicked her eyes up.

The mantle still burned. And that rotten garlic smell was stronger. Much, much stronger.

Her eyes widened. She grabbed Jade, grabbed her boots, then didn't even bother going through the doorway. She leapt through the window, hoping the snow was deep enough to cushion her fall.

The top floor of the saloon exploded.

DAIYU DIDN'T KNOW what was going on. First, she was in a dream, chasing white ghostlike rabbits through snowy forests. Then, she smelled the most awful smell, so pungent her sensitive nose burned.

And an explosion, louder than any she'd ever seen on TV.

Now she was covered with snow. Which, before now, she'd only experienced in the rabbit dream.

It was soft and fluffy but wet. And cold.

She decided she didn't like it one bit. And she missed Laila.

She could face down monsters. That's what she did, what she was born to do, sworn to do. But she missed Laila.

She wanted to go home.

She licked Dinah's face softly. Dinah laid beside her in the snow, half buried with the force of her leap. She opened her eyes, then smiled at Daiyu.

"Little Jade," Dinah said, stretching out her arms and legs, then stiffly clambering to her feet. Her boots were just a couple feet away. Dinah put them on, hopping about awkwardly to do so, then picked up Daiyu.

"Stable," Dinah said, hobbling around dazed people running out of the saloon. "We can shelter in the stable."

The hint of dawn on the horizon was dwarfed by the hungry flames devouring the roof and second floor of the Jackalope Saloon.

The heavy winter clouds, though, were gone.

The stable, out behind the saloon, was warm and quiet. A single kerosene lantern hung near the door. Dinah lit it gingerly. Nothing happened but a soft flame.

Some horses were shuffling uneasily in their stalls, but Malyu, unruffled as ever, whickered softly when she caught Dinah's scent.

Dinah figured Jade would be safe here, while she went back to the saloon to see what aid she could render. Given that it was her fault the place was half exploded to kingdom come. She wondered what Reverend Edwards would have to say about all this. Snow demons and magical beasts.

He'd probably claim it was the Lord's will if the whole place burned.

He might even say a little black dog, seen just before the saloon exploded, was an agent of Lucifer.

That sudden wrenching in her heart. Jade might not be safe, even in the stable. She might never be safe, with Dinah.

She lifted Jade up, kissed her round fluffy head. "Little one, I want you to be safe and happy. My life isn't right for a little dog, even one that turns into a lion. Can you find your way home?"

Jade licked Dinah's nose, then stared at her solemnly. Dinah double looped the fox sorcerer's charm over

Jade's neck. "Take this, as a token of my love and respect. Don't forget me. I wish you safely home," Dinah whispered, a tear trickling down her cheek.

~

I WANT TO GO HOME, Daiyu thought, whimpering as she licked Dinah's cheek, tasting her salty lonely tears. *I'm sorry, but I really miss my Laila.*

~

THE PUPPY SHIMMERED in the soft light of the lantern, then disappeared.

Dinah's hands felt so empty. But not as empty as her heart.

She trudged back to the saloon to see if she could do any good, before she had to run out of town.

~

DAIYU WAS in her spot on the green velvet sofa. Her fur, still damp from the snow, got the fabric a bit wet and dirty.

The TV was still on. Sometimes it would turn itself off, but it was still on. Daiyu squinted at the clock on the DVR.

Just after 1 a.m.

The front door banged open. Laila and Oz, laughing, bearing gift bags, carrying their coats because it was Christmas in Los Angeles, not the snow swept plateaus of 19th century Deseret.

"Daiyu, we missed you!" Laila said, gathering her up and kissing her after she'd set her bags down. "Oh, you're wet! What happened, spill your water dish?"

Daiyu nuzzled her, licking her cheek. *You couldn't even guess*, she thought.

"What's this?" Oz asked, puzzled, fingering the leather thong and charm. Daiyu eyed him suspiciously. *None of your business.* Laila couldn't see it, apparently, and that was fine with Daiyu.

"Tia Margarita said to bring you next time, she'll take some antihistamines," Laila continued, oblivious. "She sent you some special treats she made just for you." Laila fished around in one gift bag, featuring dogs dressed up like reindeer, gamboling around Christmas trees, and found a bone- shaped treat. "Here you go."

Daiyu took it delicately and nibbled, gazing up at Laila all the while. *I love you.*

"I love you, too," Laila said.

Daiyu's thoughts flashed to Dinah, so long ago and far away. *Love you too, Dinah.*

THE CURSED WOMAN

Dinah sat at the roughly carved wooden bar of the Mountain Cat Saloon and bordello in the town of Snowberry Springs, sipping on a dirty glass of warm rich whiskey.

The air was still and thick in the crowded saloon, a mix of dust and rancid body stench left over from the scorching summer day. Too early in the season for a monsoon to bring a bit of cool respite.

Dinah buried her nose in her glass, inhaling the sharp sweet bite of the whiskey, clearing her head of the stink for just a moment.

Sweat trickled down the nape of her closely shorn neck. She'd cut her thick glossy black hair short last week, and in her fringed leather jacket, thick cotton shirt, and heavy canvas trousers, she passed for a pretty mixed race boy, rather than the twenty-five old sorceress for hire and daughter of a Chinese prostitute and a fancy white Art History professor from back East.

She sat like a boy, too, legs straddling her stool, wiry form slouched over the sticky bar top.

No one would bother her, and that's how she wanted it.

She glanced at the mercury-pocked mirror behind the bar,

keeping tabs on the blurred reflections of the poker games at the various wooden tables behind her.

She marked the man in the black wool hat and trim gray wool jacket, his back to her, at the round wooden table closest to her. He was cheating, and if Dinah could pick it up just half-heartedly observing from behind in the mirror, soon enough there would be trouble. The other four men, a mix of cowhands and copper prospectors, were already glaring at Black Hat suspiciously.

Just two hands of poker and a second glass of whiskey for Dinah later, the prospector across from Black Hat hissed in anger and tossed his cards on the table, drawing a Colt 1860 as he stood up.

Dinah doubted the prospector could hit the man standing just four feet in front of him, even if the revolver had been his in the war, after all the whiskey she'd seen him drink. That didn't mean the poorly aimed bullet meant for Black Hat couldn't hit someone else.

Like her.

She slithered off the stool, head low, and slipped behind the bar, sneaky as could be, and crouched on the liquor stained wooden floor. She wanted to get upstairs anyways, and had just been killing some time before finding some excuse to unobtrusively do so.

Gnawing at a hangnail til it bled, she smeared a drop of blood on the silver *Look-Away* charm she always wore on a chain around her neck.

Dinah needed to see if Mrs Lily McGinnes's daughter was held captive or just hiding amongst the prostitutes upstairs. Either option meant her snooping around would be unwelcome.

A revolver ball whizzed over the bar, breaking the mirror and sending shards of silvered glass down on Dinah's head. She scrambled to the far end of the bar, closest to the rough wooden staircase heading upstairs, ignoring the crashing and whooping and yelling from the saloon. Just more cover for her.

Dinah dashed out to the stairs, trusting both the mayhem behind her and her *Look-Away* charm to keep attention off her. She climbed up the rickety, splintery stairs like she was scaling a cliff side, keeping low and moving swiftly and surely. Upon reaching the top, she glanced down into the saloon to see if anyone was watching.

Just one man was: Black Hat, somehow removed from the chaos he caused.

All around fists were flying, knives were stabbing, and guns were shooting, but he stood calmly. He met her gaze with brilliant amber eyes that she recognized from a job gone south a couple months ago. Coyote. He touched one finger to the brim of his black hat, smirked, then just flat out disappeared, leaving a brief afterimage of a long pointy snout and wicked sharp white teeth, red tongue lolling in canine humor, under that black hat.

Dinah cussed softly. She didn't need any misguided help from any spirits, let alone Coyote. Trouble followed him, nipping at his heels. She just wanted to get this job done. In and out, clean as can be.

Because something about this job stank.

She didn't trust Lily McGinnes and her version of the story of her runaway daughter, even at the outset, but Dinah needed the cash, both for oats for her mule and provisions for her own belly as she moved on from Deseret territory.

Dinah had a hankering to go west, maybe all the way to San Francisco. Somewhere far away from the desert, far from life-sucking fox sorcerers, water-despoiling cravens, and foreign ice demonesses. Someplace she could start a new life, her own life.

But doing that required money.

Something about Lily McGinnes had raised Dinah's hackles. Maybe it was the limpid blue eyes, soft and watery on first glance, but hard and cold as steel if you looked deeper. Maybe it was the soft, breathy drawl, sweet as iced tea as she told Dinah about seventeen-year-old Katy; but Dinah heard the venom and rage just barely under the surface.

Dinah understood a woman couldn't always be upfront about herself, had to disguise her strength, but there was a meanness that Lily just couldn't hide from Dinah.

And maybe it was the cold possessive snakey witchiness that clung to Mrs McGinnes's soul.

"Find my daughter," Lily said. "Return her to me." Those pale blue eyes blazed like the mantle of a gas lamp, incandescent but brittle. She'd held Dinah's hand so tightly Dinah's hand had ached for hours.

Servants trusted Dinah. She was more like one of them than the fancy folk they worked for.

"Grocer's son next door might know what happened," the McGinnes' cook whispered, glancing towards the front of the house. "He's doing poorly, now, like to die soon. But he and Miss Katy were close."

Dinah confronted Samuel, the grocer's son, who'd hidden Katy amongst the bags of hard wheat he'd been carting to a farm just outside the city. His lovesick eyes, warm hazel that sparked at the mention of Katy's name, told Dinah all she needed to know. He'd loved her.

"I took her to the Jevins farm," he said, hacking. His face was thin and bone white. Two hectic hot patches on his cheeks were the only spot of color on his face. "I just wisht I could have gone with her. But she asked me to stay behind and tell her mama she'd gone in the opposite direction."

Loved the girl enough to set her free.

Unlike Katy's mama, Dinah suspected, already sorry she'd taken partial payment from Mrs McGinnes to find Katy. Lily McGinnes would never set free something she figured belonged to her.

Dinah chased rumors of Lily's blonde, green eyed, freckle-nosed daughter, listening to the spirits of the cholla and juniper, the impertinent squawks of the scrub jays, the soft squeaks of the shy ringtailed miner's cats.

All the way from the McGinnes mansion in Salt Lake City to the high plateau, ramshackle cowtown of Snowberry Springs.

No duress, the spirits whispered. *The girl travels of her own free will.*

Dinah could find Katy, talk to her, let her know her mama wanted her home. That much set fine with Dinah.

But Dinah knew that the other half payment, to be paid on the return of Katy to Mrs McGinnes, might be forfeit. Dinah had to make her own mind up whether she'd haul the girl back to Salt Lake. She'd told Mrs McGinnes as much when Mrs McGinnes hired her.

Dinah tiptoed along the weathered, splintery floorboards of the hallway at the top of the stairs. Any creaks from the floor were covered by the grunts and breathy gasps filtered through the cracks between the shut doors and door frames to the small bedrooms either side of the hallway.

Shoot, Dinah didn't even have to bother to be quiet. No one up here cared about anything else beyond what was between their legs.

Gasp. Moan. Even a sob. Dinah rolled her eyes, and headed down the gas-lit hallway til she stood outside a door from behind which only came the low murmur of two different voices. None of that barn-yard talk, either.

"...leave tomorrow morning," a sweet husky voice said. "I know someone's close to finding me. I won't go back. I just won't."

Dinah gently knocked on the door, wincing as a splinter snagged her knuckle. She whispered a quick cantrip as she smeared a drop of blood from her knuckle onto the doorknob and twisted.

The lock snicked open.

Dinah didn't even clear the doorway before a five inch long iron knife thunked into the doorjamb and teetered just above her left ear.

"Well," Dinah said, plucking it out and hefting it. Nice blade, well balanced. "That's mighty inhospitable of you."

She surveyed the room's inhabitants. To her left, near the lace-curtained window, stood a young white man, dressed in stained brown trousers, scuffed brown leather boots, and a white and faded red striped buttoned shirt coated with trail muck. His thin pale face was pinched with worry.

At the foot of the wooden bed, laying on her side, propped up on one elbow, long legs stretched across the neatly made bed, lounged a young woman.

If you could call a puma lurking for just the right moment to slaughter a deer *lounging*.

Dinah bet she threw that knife, not the boy.

Glorious red hair, silky and gleaming in the gas lamplight, streamed over the girl's shoulders. Wide set brilliant green eyes, absinthe green, with all the hallucinatory promise of the color. Freckles dusted her nose and fine cheekbones.

The girl wore black wool trousers, a white men's shirt, and a leather vest, none of which hid her generous curves.

If her mother Lily was the mantle of a gas lamp, Katy was the flame itself.

No. Katy was the blazing sun to Dinah's lean crescent moon.

Never had Dinah wanted someone so desperately.

I can never, never, return this girl to Mrs McGinnes.

A sick bolt of cold vicious bitterness struck at Dinah's soul like the strike of a rattler. She collapsed to the dusty floor. Her money pouch. The attack came from it. Pulsing, vile, ripping.

Dinah's last action was to untie the pouch from her belt and feebly push it aside before everything went black.

DINAH WOKE up on the bed, fully dressed except her boots. She was stretched out perpendicular to the rough wooden headboard, stockinged feet dangling off the side. Her money pouch was propped on the window sill, far away from her as possible without tossing it out.

Sensible of the two, to understand that was part of the problem.

She felt like that time last summer her mule Malyu shied from a rattlesnake and dumped her on the ground, wind knocked out of her, dazed, and not out of danger yet.

Dim light, dawnlight, streamed through the lace curtains of the window. The sharp scent of dew-kissed desert sage slipped into the room, through the gaps between the window and the frame.

All night. Whatever that spell was, it knocked her out all night. It had the stink and venom that Dinah had felt in Mrs McGinnes. Not even the early morning sage got that out of her nose.

Katy and the young man both slept, Katy tucked up into a thread-bare armchair to the right of the window, softly snoring, the young man on the faded patched wool rug next to the bed. Blocking the doorway. Not that Dinah wanted out, yet. Her business here wasn't done.

Katy was an angel in black leather and dusty cotton, a golden nimbus around her head from the rising sun, dark gold lashes fluttering against the encroaching light.

Dinah darn well forgot to breathe, Katy was such a pretty sight.

Katy's eyes snapped open and met hers. Absinthe. Dinah was a whiskey girl, but she'd try absinthe.

"Mornin'," said Dinah quietly.

"Good morning," said Katy, her voice soft and husky and not a bit sleepy. "I think you owe me an explanation. Did my mother send you?"

Dinah appreciated folks who got straight to the point.

"She did. And I think she put a spell on the money she paid me upfront, in case I changed my mind about bringing you home to her." Dinah nodded towards the money pouch. She felt a tug, a cramp, in her gut, a promise of pain to come.

The sunlit angel was gone. The puma sat there instead, poised to attack if needed.

"I take it you've changed your mind, then?" said Katy, eyes narrowed, voice still easy. She held her knife, loosely, in her right hand. Dinah didn't know where she'd been hiding it.

"I have." Dinah paused. "I took her money to find you. I have to tell her I found you, least send word that I did. Else I'm forsworn."

Dinah didn't want to get within ten miles of Mrs Lily McGinnes ever again. But Dinah feared if she was forsworn, it wouldn't just feel like her guts were being yanked out.

She'd underestimated Mrs McGinnes. She wouldn't again.

"My mama's mean," Katy said. "She won't ever forgive you, or forget you, if you cross her."

"Figure as much. Not changin' my mind." Dinah didn't much like Salt Lake anyways. San Francisco was sounding nicer and nicer.

"I'm leaving Snowberry Springs today. Go on ahead and tell her you found me. I'll be gone before she can get here."

Rustling by the side of the bed. The young man was waking up. "Katy?" he said sleepily.

"Danny, pack up my horse and my mule, will you? And settle the bill here. Thanks, honey," she said.

Danny nodded, a lovesick look in his eyes, pulled on his boots, and left, as Katy watched pensively.

"I'm heading to San Francisco," Dinah said. "I wouldn't mind a travelling companion."

"You send word to my mother, then we get that spell off that money. Then we see about San Francisco," said Katy, a sweet smile ghosting across her full soft lips. "I'd love to see the ocean."

FAR-SPEAKING spells weren't Dinah's strength, but she had forced herself to practice over the years. She had an irregular spheroid of translucent obsidian shot with spears of clear crystalline quartz she used as a focus, safely stored in Malyu's saddle bag.

She went to the stable to fetch it.

If she couldn't *Far-Speak*, she'd simply post a letter. Mrs McGinnes might be surprised to find her bounty hunter literate, but that didn't matter. Dinah could still fulfill her the terms of her hire, leastwise what she'd been paid for.

The stable was cool and dark in the early morning, pungent with horse manure and sweet hay. Dinah could hear Danny at the far end, loading up a pack for Katy's mule, murmuring softly to the beast. The other horses rustled in their stalls. A barn cat, gray tabby with bright green eyes nearly as pretty as Katy's, wound a figure eight around Dinah's legs, almost tripping her as she gathered up Malyu's saddle bags.

Pain. A sharp stab like a knife in the kidneys. Dinah gasped, a tear trickling out of one eye despite herself.

"Just be patient, you bitch," she muttered, digging out the focus stone. It filled her palm, cool and heavy.

Dinah sat, cross-legged, in the dirt aisle running down the middle of the stable, leaning against the door of Malyu's stall. She tore at a hangnail with her teeth, smeared a dab of blood against the stone, and breathed, breathed, losing herself in the stone.

Mrs McGinnes? she projected. *Mrs Lily McGinnes?*

Something shifted, slithered, came awake. A somnolent reptile awareness focused on her, sharpening until she felt pierced by it.

Yessss? Bounty hunter? Measured surprise, recalculations.

Katy is in Snowberry Spring.

Satisfaction.

Our deal is done.

Rage blossomed, poisonous and thick, and Dinah choked back a scream. Burning, burning, in her gut. She tasted blood and bile in her mouth. *Our deal is done, fair and square, paid and fulfilled!*

BRING HER TO ME.

No! We are DONE. Dinah flung the focus stone across the aisle. It crashed against the stall door opposite, provoking a startled whinny from the stall's occupant.

Dinah clutched her stomach, then leaned over and wrapped her arms around her legs, sobbing. It hurt so bad. Like someone cutting out her insides with a dull knife, then dowsing it all with acid.

She forced herself to think through the miasma pulsing through her veins. She had to get back up to Katy's room, get that damn hurt off the money. But first she wanted to dig through that bag of charms she'd taken from a fox sorcerer a few months back. See if there was anything in there that could help somehow with getting the spell off the money.

"Need a hand, darlin'?" Coyote leaned over the stall door opposite that the focus stone had hit. A pretty palomino mare, the stall's talkative occupant, stood behind him and nipped at his silky dark hair.

"Shoo, you," he said to the mare. "I know I'm in your stall, but it's my stall now."

The mare ignored him, closing her eyes and nibbling a bit more.

"Shucks," he said, "it's that lavender water Miss Jilly at the bordello uses. Rinsed my hair with it. This blonde little gal can't resist it."

He leered at Dinah. "Most gals can't." He puffed out his chest, leanly muscled under a white cotton shirt with silver and turquoise cufflinks, charcoal grey wool vest, and black wool jacket with silver buttons. His black wool hat was pulled low over his amber eyes, but he flashed a bright toothy smile at Dinah.

Dinah didn't know if his presence shielded her from Mrs McGinnes, or if it was just her exasperation, but she didn't hurt quite so much.

"Care to exchange some money?" she asked. Dinah figured Coyote could deal with Mrs McGinnes. Give that nasty snake a surprise, Lily tried to bite Coyote.

"You'll owe me, darlin'. Is it worth that much to you?" He vaulted over the stall door and landed in a crouch right in front of her, silver spurs on his black leather boots jangling softly, picking up her focus stone and handing it to her. He touched her belly, just above her waistband.

"My, my," he said, eyes suddenly grave. "You are hurtin'. You don't want to incur the debt this would be worth." Damn coyote.

"I need my charm bag," she said. She had a *Protection* charm, a new brass-plated mountain lion tooth, that might, just might, work, even on the coins, if she gave it enough blood. Safer than one of the untried charms from the fox sorcerer. At this point she didn't care if the *Protection* charm destroyed the coins, rather than just removing the spell.

Another stab of pain, two, three, four, a snake striking to make sure she caused mortal harm. Sobbing, Dinah dug through Malyu's saddle bags, found the doeskin charm bag, then the mountain lion charm.

Coyote held her left hand steady as she sliced through the meat of the base of her thumb, letting blood coat the tooth til it blazed like a storm-warning sunrise, red and orange and scarlet.

She clutched the charm in her throbbing, spasming left hand.

The pain in her abdomen disappeared.

Dinah could hear, just under the perception of audible sound, an enraged hiss.

Poisonous energy, vile and viscous, bounced along the backs of the stabled horses, testing the aura of each, til it landed at the feet of Danny, humming tunelessly as he groomed a pretty black paint mare, lost in his own dreams of a red-headed girl, oblivious to Dinah or Coyote.

It tasted him and struck.

He didn't even cry out as he slumped to the ground. Stone dead.

Dinah scrambled up, wrapping a kerchief around her left hand, snugging the charm against the still-weeping wound. "No, no, no."

Coyote grabbed her arm, keeping her from running to the young man.

"He's dead. Nothin' you can do, darlin', except keep your head about you and get the hell out of here. Who they gonna blame for this? You."

She shrugged him off. "I need to tell Katy."

KATY WAS PACING back and forth in front of the window, anxiously glancing outside towards the stable, when Dinah entered the room.

And stopped, dumbstruck.

Where was the glorious sunlit angel? This girl was pretty enough, with muted auburn hair, hazel eyes tending towards bottle green, and a coltish figure that didn't do much to fill out the men's trousers, shirt, and vest she wore.

But far from the Botticelli vision of before.

"Katy?" Dinah said.

The young woman registered Dinah's reaction, glanced at Dinah's blood stained wrapped hand. She couldn't meet Dinah's eyes.

"I'm sorry," Dinah whispered. "Danny's dead."

"I know. I felt it. Same as I felt my mama attacking you first. Told you she was spiteful."

"What did you do to us? To me?"

"I can't help it. I'm cursed."

"What did you do, Katy?" Dinah's hand—*no*, the mountain lion tooth charm—pulsed briefly. Katy whimpered, and her hair dulled further.

"My mama lay with a *gancanagh*. A lovetalker. My da. I inherited some of his power," said Katy. "I don't mean to use it. I really don't. But if I'm scared, I can't help it. And my mama wants me to use my powers, for the family. For her. That's why I ran away."

Dinah could easily picture Mrs McGinnes offering her daughter to the wealthy scions of Salt Lake, given the slightest hope of gain.

And she'd heard about these lovetalkers from her schol-arly papa. "Lovetalkers make people fall in love with them. Then they kill them."

"Not on purpose!" Katy said. "And not right away. If I leave them, they're fine, after a while."

Dinah didn't know if that was true or just Katy's wishful thinking, remembering the lovesick grocer's boy, wasting away. Didn't matter. Dinah was done with the girl.

Coins spraying across the woolen coverlet as she dumped the contents of her money pouch.

She methodically picked up each coin with her wrapped hand and concentrated.

Some coins lay in her hand, inert.

But with each bespelled coin, she felt a tug on her hand and a new spurt of blood soaking through the wrap coating the lion tooth charm. Each tainted coin melted into a stinking sick vapor that wisped away to nothing.

Much as she both feared and expected, using the mountain lion tooth.

She was left with a bare handful of copper pennies and a couple nickels, and feeling a mite light headed with all the blood loss.

"You can't leave me," Katy said, panic turning that husky voice to a whine.

"I can and I will. Be glad I'm leaving you alive."

Dinah poured the pennies and nickels back into her money pouch, tied it to her belt, then left the room.

It would have to be enough. She'd get to San Francisco somehow.

Maybe Coyote would travel with her a ways.

And she had her beloved Malyu.

It would have to be enough.

THE JACKRABBIT GIRL

The dark skies overhead were clear, not a cloud to haze the moon.

But, looking over her shoulder back through the tiny gap between the slot canyon walls, Dinah could see heavy dark thunderheads on the horizon and a flash of lightning. The crack of thunder bounced along the canyon walls.

Electricity and creosote stung her nose, and the little hairs on her arms stood at attention.

Last thing she wanted was for her and her mule Malyu to get caught up in a flash flood.

They might not live through it to regret it.

Dinah clucked to Malyu, the sound echoing off the sides of the slot canyon, its water-stained, red-striped walls gray in the soft moonlight. She could touch those walls with each boot tip, the canyon was so narrow. But off to the right, shadows switchbacking up the wall, there looked to be a rough rocky path up out of the canyon.

Malyu swiveled a long furry ear back to her, then laboriously turned, scraping her muscular haunches—and Dinah's knees—on the walls. Malyu splashed ice cold water onto Dinah's trousers just to make sure she'd gotten her point across to Dinah, and started up the path.

Malyu was clever and sure-footed, with mind of her own. If she sensed something unsafe, she would dig in and not budge, no matter how Dinah encouraged her. That said, she had a lazy streak a mile wide, and hated climbing uphill, let alone on a path with sharp rocks to bruise her feet. Malyu preferred the soft sand of the creek bed.

Dinah couldn't blame her. They'd had a hard day, today, travelling nearly ten miles through the high desert until they reached the web of slot canyons and creeks early this evening.

Just a half mile further, and the canyon opened up to a small valley where they could camp.

Day after that, they'd be in Cottonwood Springs, where a job was awaiting Dinah, one that might get her enough cash to get her to San Francisco. Her mama, before she died, had told Dinah about a Chinese sorcerer living there who owed a debt to their family. Dinah intended on cashing in on that debt, trading it for learning and, if she was lucky, a new community.

She'd been alone for too many years since her parents passed, mama from yellow fever and her papa from a broken heart. She wanted a home, away from prejudice.

Regardless, it looked like she and Malyu would have to camp elsewhere, now.

Two precarious switchbacks later, Dinah heard a warning rumble. A blast of wind knocked her black wool hat straight off, the cord straining across her throat the only thing keeping it from flying down the canyon.

Malyu froze, then bolted up the path til it narrowed so much she had to stop or plummet off the side.

They weren't ten feet above the creek, its formerly ice clear waters turning cloudy with mud.

Dinah would dismount, just so they could get a few feet further, but there wasn't any room.

The thunderheads scudded across the full moon, turning the moon red. Dinah saw two huge shadows, darting in and out of the clouds, lightning sparking from their wingtips. Thunderbirds. Their bass cries shook the air, breaking sandstone outcrops into showers of red and cream sand, filling Dinah's hat brim and trickling down the back of her shirt.

She didn't even notice the itching.

The rumble was now the roar of a steam train barreling down a hill, brakes useless against gravity and momentum. Nothing could stop it.

A wall of muddy water roared down the canyon towards them, trees and boulders tossed around within it. The logs splintered against the sides of the canyon. One shot up next to her and Malyu, hitting Dinah's leg with an agonizing crack.

Dinah didn't have time to be thankful it hit her, not Malyu, before the second broken log rebounded against the opposite side of the canyon and smacked her in the head.

A SWEET FURRED FACE, long ears draping down like pigtails from under a straw hat with a red and cream silk polka dotted band, gazed down into hers. Dinah smelled the soft musk of something wild. Clean, but wild.

Dinah closed her eyes, opened them, squinted.

The face was still there, still furry, but now smiling. The early morning sunlight caught silver highlights in its fur. Besides the dainty straw hat, the creature wore a gingham blouse and a long cotton skirt, decorated with fine ivory lace tatting along the hem. She looked like a jackrabbit crossed with a person, standing tall on two bare long narrow feet, with lanky human-shaped limbs and body.

"You're awake," she said, stroking Dinah's hair back with a delicate hand, soft with silvery grey fur like that on its face.

"Is Malyu alright?" Dinah rasped. Her throat hurt. Shoot, her head hurt like the dickens. Let alone her arms, her chest, and her legs. She was on the ground, on a blanket laid down on sweet-smelling grass warming in the rising sun. A second blanket, gray wool with a black and cream geometric design woven in, draped over her. She could sense the spells woven into the blanket, nibbling at the edge of her consciousness. Healing and warmth.

She still wore the same clothes from the day before, a heavy white cotton men's shirt, brown trousers, a black wool jacket, and thick woolen socks, mended time and again. All of it stuck against her skin, clammy and cold despite the blanket. She touched her head gingerly. Her black hair, growing out since she'd hacked it boyishly short last winter, was matted and sticky with blood.

Her skull seemed intact, at least, even if her flesh wasn't.

She tried to sit up and yelped.

"Stay still," admonished the creature. "Let me help you." She was small but strong, as she effortlessly lifted Dinah up to a sitting position.

Dinah was used to seeing Coyote in all his forms, from that of a hungry scrawny coyote to a coyote-headed human to a fully human-appearing creature. She figured, as her mind unfogged, that this woman was something similar.

"Not a god," the jackrabbit girl said. "My name's Mary.

Just a jackrabbit."

"With power enough to look into my mind," Dinah said suspiciously.

"Just the surface. We're prey. Need some sort of protection. And yes, your mule is fine. Bruised, and hungry, but fine." Mary cocked her head. "Can you eat something?"

Bile soured her mouth. "No," Dinah said.

Mary's nose twitched, furrowing her brow. "That's not good," she said. "You hit your head awfully hard."

"I remember the thunderbirds—" Dinah said. To be frank, her brain felt like them swooping through the storm, 'cept her brain was rattling against her skull, not the stormclouds.

"I think you need to see William," Mary said. "He doesn't like your kind, but he's a healer, and healin' is what he must do." Mary stood, then leaned over and scooped Dinah up like she was a helpless kitten.

~

William looked completely human, with a broad tanned face and narrow amber eyes. His barrel chest strained the leather vest, accented with turquoise and onyx beading, that he wore over nothing but his bare skin. A mass of amulets—carved stone, bits of bone, leather wrapped feathers—hung from leather cords around his neck. Loose cotton trousers covered his bottom half, for which Dinah was grateful. His feet, like Mary's, were bare, with thick curling toenails at the end of his hairy toes.

If Dinah squinted, those toes blurred together into hooves. Or maybe it was just her poor swollen brain not working quite right.

Dinah figured the "your kind" William disliked meant human, not Chinese. As the daughter of a Chinese prostitute sorceress and a white Art History professor, living on her own as a sorceress for hire, she faced enough bigotry in her daily life. Piling on one more instance of prejudice didn't matter much.

Mary had brought her to a small cottonwood lean-to fitted out with a pallet with more gray wool blankets next to a small iron-strapped wooden trunk. Mary deposited Dinah on the palette, adjusting the blankets so Dinah was covered chin to toes, then tucked one more blanket, tightly rolled, under her neck and head.

"You sure about this, Mary?" asked William.

"You tell me, William. What's gonna happen if we don't?" Mary gave Dinah a quick kiss on the forehead, then left.

A dull, dinged-up metal pot sat on top of some flat rocks next to a fire pit out in front of the lean to. Earthy steam with just a hint of sweetness wafted over to her, mingling with sage from the banked fire.

"Brewed up some tea," William said, ladling some from the pot into a tin cup, and handing it to Dinah. He crossed his arms across his thick chest and scowled. "Drink it."

She did so, gagging. Didn't taste a darn bit like what it smelled. Tasted like Malyu's saddle blanket smelled, after a long day's ride.

He ducked a cotton rag into the tea and stomped back over to her. He dripped warm tea onto her face, carving rivulets in the sandstone caked into her pores, while brusquely poking around the top of her head. He grunted, then pressed the rag against her wound.

It burned, worse than the time she'd dug into a bee hive looking for honey and instead found a nest of wasps. They'd swarmed, and she'd ran, but not fast enough to avoid getting stung. She could feel them buzzing and stabbing inside her skull, stinging her again and again, until her brain turned into poisoned jelly in her skull. She screamed, and William shoved a thin cottonwood branch into her mouth crossways.

"Bite down," he said, then pressed again, squeezing the rag til all the tea was wrung out.

She complied, back arching against the agony, until she just couldn't anymore, and everything went white then black.

"You didn't have to hurt her so much," a soft voice complained.

"Did what I had to. Did what you asked me to."

Dinah opened her eyes. Mary's sweet bunny face was above hers again, this time with her jaw set stubbornly and her soft brown eyes angry. Fierce little rabbit.

Dinah groaned, and both Mary and William looked down at her, Mary hopeful, William irritated.

"How do you feel?" Mary asked.

Dinah considered. "Better than I expected," she said.

William harrumphed and stomped off. Dinah thought she heard the thunk of hooves against the sandstone.

"William said you won't die, now. He thought you might've, if I'd not found you and brought you here and let him take care of you."

"Where is here, anyways?" Besides the lean to, she could see other structures, some more permanent like the log cabin twenty yards away, others simply canvas stretched over poles to provide a bit of shade. She could see a few jackrabbity folks like Mary tending to some corn, as well as larger people with hints of horns curling around their heads doing various homely tasks.

"Harmony Crossing," Mary said. "Just this side of the Dream World. I heard your mule braying after the flood, and found you both."

"Found me like that?" Dinah eyed Mary's floppy ears.

If a rabbit could blush, Mary did, her silvery fur darkening to rose. "Like this," the jackrabbit girl said, features morphing to those of a tan slender girl with strong white teeth, long grey and black hair tied up in tail streaming down her back.

Dinah nodded. "Smart," she said, and Mary's eyes brightened. Dinah sat up fully, pushing the blanket to the side. "How good are William's potions, anyhow? Good enough I can get going?"

Dinah figured, halfway into the Dream World or not, she couldn't be too far off her trail. She could still make it to Cottonwood Springs by nightfall, if Malyu was sound.

"Going?" Mary asked. "Where are you going?"

"I got a job lined up, honey, one that can make me enough money to get to San Francisco."

Mary clutched Dinah's hands, human hands shifting back to slender hand-like paws. "You can't go," she whispered. "You can't ever leave."

"Course I can," Dinah said, drawing back her hands. "I thank you for your kindness, and I do owe you a debt for caring for me, but I need to leave."

"That tea that William gave you? The magic in that tea, in the water, it won't last if you leave. You'll die if you go back to your world."

Dinah stared at her, stricken. *They took away her choice*? "You didn't even ask me. You just did it."

"I had to, Dinah. I couldn't let you die."

"That's for me to decide, not you," Dinah said, shaking her head. "Go. Just go. I don't want to see any bit of your rabbity face right now."

Mary sobbed, then dashed away, her fleet-footedness at odds with her dainty hat and skirts.

How could Mary? How could she have done this to Dinah? The one thing, the one thing that Dinah embraced, was her own self sufficiency and agency.

She had to find William. Had to find out if she had any options.

HE WASN'T in the settlement. "Go to the springs," folks told her. "You'll find him there."

To the springs, then. Likely the source of this magical water that would keep her here, halfway between her world and the Dream World.

The tea had worked. Her head felt clear, like she'd slept soundly and deeply. No more angry wasps stinging the tarnation out of her. She remembered the branch hitting her shin, the bone deep crack, the numbness after the jolt of pain. Her leg felt fine now, no swelling or bruising, as she walked amongst the cottonwoods up the narrow valley. Even that crick in her neck she got after riding all day, that never went away til she had a couple days off Malyu's back, that was even gone.

She'd take that crick, and the injured leg, even the wasp-stung jelly brain, if it bought her freedom.

The trees grew together thicker and arched overhead, sun dappling the dusty sandstone path rather than beating down upon it. A soft burble reached her ears. A minerally tang twitched her nose.

William crouched next to the tiny spring, just a yard or so across, filling a water bag with the clear water. His feet were hooves, now, shiny and black, and thick glossy tan horns curled back and around his pointed ears.

"Knew you'd come looking for me," he said, amber goat eyes meeting hers. "Knew Mary made a mistake. That girl just doesn't think before she acts."

"She said I can't leave."

"Got someplace better to be?"

"I don't know about better," Dinah said. "I just know I have someplace I'm choosin', rather than being forced, to be."

He nodded. "I respect that. Problem is, respect doesn't mean a thing against facts."

"Will I die?"

"Maybe, maybe not. More likely maybe, though. That crack on your head broke something inside. Else fixing it wouldn't have hurt so bad."

"I can't stay here."

"It's safe," William said. "Plenty to eat, the weather's mild, folks are friendly."

Dinah thought of the thunderbirds, soaring in the winds, lightning sparking off their wings. "Safety and comfort are agreeable," she said. "But I want to fly."

He nodded. "Thought so. There's even a shaman you could learn from, if you wanted. Healing magics. It's safe here, but accidents and sickness still occur. You'd be a valued member of the settlement."

"That's not me," Dinah said, heart sinking. For just a moment, she wished it *could* be her. But there was so much else she wanted to learn. More about her mama's people. More about *her* people.

"Figured that. You're a hard one, Dinah." He untied an amulet, a small carved rainbow obsidian thunderbird, dangling from a leather cord, from around his neck, then looped it around hers, knotting it snugly. "Take this. Don't ever take it off. Come back in three years, after you've learned what you need to. I'll teach you how to manipulate and use the healing water. Then we'll discuss terms. You do owe us."

"You'll let me leave?"

He shrugged. "Leaving's not the issue. Keeping your brains from leaking out that hard skull of yours is. That amulet will link you to us, maintain the potency of the healing. Won't last forever, though, so don't try to cheat the time."

"Thank you," Dinah said.

"Don't thank me. Thank that poor little jackrabbit whose heart you're breaking."

MARY WAS WAITING for her at the edge of the settlement, Malyu's reins in one furred hand. "I'm sorry, I'm sorry," she said. "But I couldn't let you die—"

"Don't you worry, Mary. I understand." To Mary, was Dinah a thunderbird? Dinah thought so, from the longing in Mary's eyes. "I don't like the circumstances, that's all. And I'll be back in three years, for William to teach me."

She mounted Malyu, who turned her head to nuzzle Dinah's knee. "How do I leave, Mary?"

"Just want to," Mary said. "Just fix it in your mind, and Malyu will take you."

Dinah nodded, then nudged Malyu forward, toward the far end of the valley. She closed her eyes.

When she opened them, Mary and Harmony Crossing had disappeared. Dinah was in the small valley she'd intended on camping in the night before. Just a day's ride to Cottonwood Springs.

She squeezed her legs and Malyu trotted ahead.

Three years. She had three years of freedom.

THE CURANDERA

Dinah, half Chinese, half white, sorceress for hire, lay with her belly flat on the smooth dirt floor of the one-room jailhouse in the town of Jackalope Wash, Deseret Territory. She didn't dare twitch a muscle.

A tiny, white scorpion scuttled back and forth in front of her face, quartz shard stinger twitching above its back, a tiny drip of venom dangling from said stinger. The hypnotic desert rose scent of the venom wafted towards her, wooing her with tales of sweet dreams of her heart's desire.

The back of her skull, swollen and tender, throbbed with each step the scorpion took. Morning light, streaming from the tiny clerestory windows, jabbed into her poor rattled brain like a lightning strike. The early morning bustle on the street, donkeys and mules braying, men swearing at each other, the rumble of a stagecoach bucking along the mud-pitted main street, was a broom handle thwacking against her skull.

The soured cream in the coffee? That sticky acidic sweet taste in her mouth. Dinah expected she must've vomited several times over the night, not that she remembered a damn thing.

The scorpion gathered itself up in a fit of bravado, fully intending to make an end of this standoff.

The thought of rolling out of its way brought up more bile.

"Hold still," a sweet contralto voice said from behind her. "Ven aqui, mi linda, come here."

The scorpion paused, now mere inches from Dinah's nose. Dinah's eyes crossed, trying to keep the creature in focus. She could see the indecision in its beady little eyes, all ten of 'em, two atop its head and four pair along the side of its head. How it wanted to sting her, and feed off the energy of her lonely dreams. How hungry it was.

It scuttled away and behind her, towards the woman calling it.

Dinah let out her breath.

"Can you sit up?"

"I'm sure I can," Dinah said, voice raspy and dry. "Not sure I want to."

She pushed up with her arms, quivering like a newborn colt, then got her feet up under her. Despite wanting to fall back to the hard-packed dirt, she slapped at her canvas trousers, stained with gods only knew what, and brushed off her white cotton shirt. What used to be white, anyhow. She still wore her blunt toed leather boots. Errant wisps of her thick straight hair, pulled back in a long tail streaming down her back, tickled her face.

All her amulets, usually strung on a leather cord hung around her neck, were missing, including one meant to keep her healed from an otherwise mortal injury, a blow from a branch against her temple, incurred several months ago.

One reason her head must hurt so darn much.

Hard as she tried, she had no recollection of getting hit on the back of the head, or being tossed into the jailhouse, or even why she had been tossed into the jailhouse.

She turned to look at her cell companion.

The woman cupped the scorpion in one tanned hand. Silver and turquoise rings on each finger weighed her hands down. Silver cuffs, inscribed with arcane symbols, encircled her sturdy wrists. If Dinah squinted, the symbols danced along the surfaces of the bracelets. Enchanted.

The scorpion looked mighty comfortable, tail relaxed, like it was home.

"He is trapped, like us," the woman said.

"Just keep it away from me," Dinah said.

The woman smirked. "Mi nombre es Jacquelinda. Yours?"

"Dinah." She didn't trust this woman. To be honest, she couldn't think of one person she trusted, so that was nothing unusual.

Jacquelinda was tall, a good four inches taller than Dinah, with full curves and a nipped in waist, accentuated by full black skirts and an embroidered blouse cinched with a wide leather belt. Multiple pouches hung off that belt, full of gods only knew what. Her plain face was dark, both from sun and birth, with soft cheeks, deep brown eyes, and full rosy lips. Her sensuous black curls, half pinned, half loose, cascaded over her shoulders.

She wore practical boots like Dinah's, sturdy leather with rounded toes and stacked leather heels for staying in the stirrups, but stitched with symbols, scarlet thread bright against the dull brown, unlike Dinah's plain boots.

"Bruja," whispered Dinah. *Witch*.

"Curandera," corrected Jacquelinda. *Healer*.

Dinah snorted. "Why'd they let you keep all your spelled items?"

"No one here but you has the eyes to see them." She shrugged. "Happily for the both of us."

"You can get us out?" Dinah surveyed the room. Thick solid adobe walls enclosed the ten by ten foot room, a heavy wooden door with an iron lock on the west wall the only practical entrance or exit. Clerestory windows along the east wall let sunlight and fresh air (though the aroma of manure and piss from the street was rising with the morning heat).

A chamber pot sat in the southeast corner, and a jug of what Dinah assumed was water in the northeast corner. She helped herself to a swig of what was indeed warm dusty water, swishing it around her mouth before swallowing. She winced. Her *head*.

"Chew these," Jacquelinda said, fishing a couple pieces of bark out of one pouch. "They'll help with the pain."

Dinah popped the bark into her mouth. Nasty and bitter, but she felt the pressure in her head slacking. Willow bark. Maybe the curandera had earned a smidgen of trust.

"And yes, I think I can get us out," Jacquelinda said. She snagged a plain hairpin out of her hair and bent before the lock, sticking in the hairpin and wiggling it around.

Why do magic, when simple skills of thievery would suffice?

"I need my amulets," Dinah said.

Jacquelinda glanced back over her shoulder. "I would say you don't, but as long as you believe you do, you certainly will."

Definitely a medicine woman, not a witch. Only medicine folk spoke thus, in convoluted self important statements.

Dinah heard the heavy snick of the lock opening.

"There's a building next door, to the left," Jacquelinda said. "Belongs to the sheriff. His office, a meeting room, a place for him and the occasional deputy to bunk as needed. Your amulets will be there.

"As will be the evil man you tried, and failed, to kill."

Luckily, the doorway from the jailhouse opened away from the main street. Unfortunately, this back alley still had a steady flow of folks rushing along on errands.

Dinah possessed a *Look-Away* amulet, but it did her little good right now, given it was locked up away from her with the rest of her amulets.

"Think of yourself unnoticed," hissed Jacquelinda. She shimmered in the morning sun, her stately form flickering, til she looked like a hunched, obsequious old woman. She scuttled away from the jailhouse doorway to the similar one-storied adobe structure to the left, and brazenly opened the wooden door and walked right in like she belonged.

Dinah's head throbbed. She'd once had a run in with a fox sorcerer, a handsome Chinaman with a streak of evil arrogance a mile wide. He and his pair of sandy foxes waltzed down the center of a bustling main street full of folks, and no one else even noticed them 'cept her.

Her head pounded. If she concentrated—

She stepped out into the alley, avoiding a pile of steaming horse manure, and wove her way through the crowd, clenching her fists and grinding her teeth. Folks parted like she was a boulder in creek, like it was natural to flow around her.

Just four steps more, three, two, one. She pressed her forehead against the cool adobe wall, the main door to the right, panting, then straightened and entered the building.

Unlike the jailhouse, it possessed multiple rooms and a pine wooden floor. This first room, stretching the length of the building, was the sheriff's workplace. A solid oak desk stacked with accounting logs and other paperwork cluttered the center of the room. A couple rickety chairs sat in front of the desk. A larger chair with a worn brown wool cushion padding the seat occupied on the other side.

Jacquelinda dug away with her hairpin at the lock of an iron-covered, wooden Allerton's strongbox, tucked against the wall behind the desk.

The wall opposite the entrance had two doorways, each leading to, Dinah assumed, a different room.

Through one of those doorways was the man she couldn't remember trying to kill.

Dinah had seen plenty of death. Her parents, and so many others, from illness. Some folks from violence. Some that she had killed herself, though she hated having to do so, even if they deserved it.

So she was sore perplexed as to why she'd ended up in a small town jailhouse for trying to kill some stranger. And what he'd done to incur her vengeful nature.

Whatever it was, had to be bad. Real bad.

Burning sage wafted over to her, and she glanced back, squinting against the pang that shot through her head.

Jaquelinda's hairpin alone wasn't sufficing. The curandera had lit a bundle of sage on fire and was waving it around the lock on the safe, muttering all the while in Spanish.

Nothing Dinah could do. Either Jacquelinda opened the strongbox, or she didn't. It looked heavy, but Dinah might be able to take the whole darned thing with her and open it later.

She opened the doorway to the left. It was empty except for an iron bed dressed with a faded quilt and a small carved pine wardrobe.

The doorway to the right, then.

She cracked the door open and stuck her head in. This room mirrored the other, 'cept there was a tall lanky figure tucked up under this room's quilt, with a shock of gray-streaked red hair sticking out from under the quilt.

The man murmured sleepily, then turned over to face her, the quilt falling back to his chest. From the front he looked younger than his hair, with lean freckled cheekbones, a slender nose, and a prominent Adam's apple. He opened his eyes, bright blue, hectic with fever, and reached out a trembling thin hand when he saw Dinah.

She'd never seen him before in her life.

"WHAT DID HE DO?" Dinah asked Jacquelinda. The red haired man was still on the bed, too weak to call for help, let alone get up and follow Dinah out of the room. The curandera still worked on the strongbox, cursing to herself softly in Spanish. Dinah sat on the desk, keeping an eye out for the sheriff.

"Raped and murdered my daughter," Jacquelinda said flatly, not looking at Dinah. "I hired you to find him and kill him. You agreed. Except you got yourself knocked on the back of the head last night trying to get to him and can't remember a darned thing."

Surely, if that man had done something so evil, Dinah wouldn't forget? Surely, if she'd sworn to kill someone, she wouldn't forget?

Her head hurt so bad.

"Do you have any more of that bark?" Dinah asked.

The curandera reached into a pouch and retrieved two more pieces. "Chew these. They'll help with the pain."

Dinah popped them into her mouth and chewed. Sure enough, her pain faded, and her head cleared. She shifted the bark to the side of her mouth. "Your daughter Adelina. I remember now. I'm so sorry."

Adelina had been raped and murdered, her body mutilated. By that man. Niall McGee. Wrath burned through the last of the pain in her skull.

"Go take care of that man while you still can," Jacquelinda said. "Keep chewing on those pieces of bark, though. They'll help with the pain."

Dinah nodded and obediently chewed.

THE MAN WAS SITTING UP, pale bare chest scarred scarlet with fern-like traceries. Lightning-kissed.

"Dinah?" he said, voice raw. "Dinah, what happened?"

"You raped her daughter Adelina. You murdered her," Dinah said. She clutched her head and staggered, banging her shins on the iron bed frame. Her head hurt so bad. She chewed frantically on the bark, sitting in her mouth like a drowned waterlogged rabbit, mushy and soft.

"Dinah, Adelina was my wife. She died in childbirth, cursed by her mama for trying to leave her and her sorcery," Niall said. "I hired you to protect me while we hunted her mama. I wasn't strong enough to fight her on my own."

He touched his scarred chest. "She nearly killed me. You warded me against her sorcery, using these scars."

A million fire ants chewed on her brain, a bald red-headed turkey vulture ripped out chunks of tissue, a buckskin mustang mare bucked and kicked and danced on her skull.

Dinah tried to choke back the howl rising in her throat. She exhaled, breath shrill.

And she spat out the bark.

And she *remembered*.

~

JACQUELINDA APPEARED IN THE DOORWAY. "Is it done? I heard something—"

"It's not done, hechicera malvada, you lying piece of cow dung," Dinah said, stalking towards her, desperately wishing she had her amulets. Her knife. Anything. "Hechicera malvada. Evil sorceress. You're no curandera. Your own daughter?"

The hechicera stumbled back. "Dinah, what lies did he tell you?"

Dinah didn't see the scorpion lurking the other side of the doorway until she was all the way through.

It wasn't tiny any more.

It was the size of a newborn calf, and growing. Its stinger, bigger than a railroad spike, oozed desert rose scented venom.

Dinah's vision swam. She saw her mama, her eyes alight with love, holding her hands out for the kitten Dinah had rescued.

"He's so precious," her mama whispered to her, her mama's voice soft and husky, cuddling the striped orange and cream kitten against her cheek. "Look, Patrick, at what Dinah found."

Dinah's father appeared next to her mother, reading glasses perched on his beaky nose, brown hair prematurely graying. He stroked the kitten's head. "What a wonderful kitten."

"Some boys were trying to hurt him," Dinah announced. Her left eye purpled as she spoke. "They were bigger than me, but I didn't care. You shouldn't hurt anything helpless. Not a kitten, not a person, no one."

"I'm so proud of you, Dinah," her father said.

"I'll always take care of those who need help," Dinah said. Her head ached. "No matter what the cost."

Dinah's eyes snapped open. The scorpion had crept closer during her vision, its stinger cocked and quivering.

Concentrate. The hechicera lied, but Dinah *had* crossed the alley without being seen.

The scorpion's tail flashed forward.

Dinah yanked out the memories of the lightning strike scar, her magical ward overlaying it, and thrust those memories at the scorpion.

A sharp sweet smell overwhelmed the rose-scented venom as lightning hit the scorpion. It screamed, steam hissing from under its carapace. It scuttled at her, stinger trembling, before it burst into white hot flame.

Dinah lurched away.

Where was Jacquelinda?

Niall clutched the door frame, his scars fading as the scorpion burned. "Behind you," he said.

Dinah turned.

Her head hurt like someone taking an axe to a log. "Stop that," Dinah gritted.

Jacquelinda cowered in front of her. Gone was the confident woman.

"Please, por favor, do not hurt me. I'm just an old woman, with no children. Your head hurts, doesn't it? I can help you. I'm a curandera, a healer." Jacquelinda scrabbled at the pouch on her belt, withdrew a handful of bark chips in one age-spotted bony hand. Old. Helpless.

"You lie," Dinah said.

And—the pain!—like her skull kicked in, brain matter leaching out.

The lightning! She *reached* for the lightning, even as the last of the scars faded from Niall's chest.

One last strike.

The lightning flared and coalesced into a bright burning ball, so bright Dinah thought her eyes melted and ran. Dinah screamed.

The lightning ball hit Jacquelinda square in the chest, her embroidered blouse catching fire first, then her shiny black curls, then the rest of her.

Dinah collapsed.

"Took you long enough," Niall said from the other room.

Dinah twitched open an eye. She was tucked under the quilt in the sheriff's room. Her skull was intact and her eyes clear. She was just tired, so tired.

"You told me Jacquelinda Herrera was a powerful sorceress," another man's voice said. "I sent for reinforcements who deal with her sort, since she'd shanghai'd your protector."

Dinah untangled herself from the quilt then stood up. She still wore her trousers and shirt, but her feet were bare against the smooth pine floor.

"I'm awake," she called, dragging herself into the main room.

Afternoon sunlight streamed through the windows, highlighting the occupants of the room as well as the remains of the battle.

The sheriff lounged back in his chair, a tall bulky man with long grey hair tied back in a tail. His face was lined by the sun and age and worry. The silver star on his chest gleamed, more than the sunlight warranted.

Niall sat in one of the rickety chairs. The other chair had burnt up along with Jacquelinda. All that remained of her was a greasy stain on the floor. Melted blobs of silver from her bracelets and rings stuck to the floorboards.

A similar greasy spot, the remains of the scorpion, was off to her left. Just a whiff of desert rose...then that dissipated too.

"I'd like my amulets," she said to the sheriff. "And that silver."

"Sure enough, Miss Dinah," the sheriff said. He used a small knife to cut a nick in his finger, then smeared that on the lock of the strongbox. It popped open, and the sheriff handed over the pouch of amulets, as well as the several amulets dangling from leather cords.

Dinah looped those around her neck right away, her *Healing* amulet, the *Look-Away* charm, the others. The last of her headache faded.

"How'd she get me?" she asked Niall. "I remember everything, but what happened yesterday."

"I can guess," the sheriff offered. "You and Niall rode into town yesterday afternoon like the hounds of hell were on your heels and got two rooms at the boarding house. Niall here stayed holed up, but that woman arrived on the evening stagecoach out of Mexicatl Junction. You'd gone to the saloon, and so had she. Folks told me the two of you met at the faro table, and after a bit the two of you were acting like best friends.

"Then you went upstairs and tried to kill young Niall. That point, we arrested you. Sorry about the knock on the back of your head. You put up quite the fight. We tossed you in the jail, and brought Niall here for safekeeping. He was acting sickish, and Mrs Mayweather wanted him out of the boarding house."

"But Jaquelinda—"

"I figure she joined you in the jailhouse of her own accord at some point."

"She couldn't get past your ward, Dinah," Niall said. "She needed you to bypass it yourself."

It sounded logical. Faro? Dinah wasn't a gambler, never had been, but she was ensorcelled by that point. She shuddered. To be taken over, to not have control?

"Now, Miss Dinah, I'm surely grateful you took care of that woman for us," the sheriff continued, "but folks here don't abide with foreign sorceresses."

"You need me to leave?" Dinah asked.

"Yes, miss, we do. You're fine staying the night here tonight, but tomorrow as the sun rises, you need to far from Jackalope Springs."

Niall took her hand. "Thank you, Dinah," he said. "Thank you for fighting her. For avenging Adelina and our baby." He pressed a small pouch into her hand. "What we agreed upon, and a little more."

Dinah nodded. It had to be enough.

~

THE NEXT MORNING, the sun skimming the eastern horizon and turning the sky into a riot of pink and purple and gold, Dinah mounted up on her mule Malyu, her amulets safely around her neck, or in the doeskin pouch off her belt.

Malyu's saddlebags jingled, Niall's coins and Jacquelinda's silver nestled into them.

She clucked to her and Malyu broke into a bone jarring trot. Out of Jackalope Springs. To the west.

She had a long day's ride ahead of her, though she wasn't quite sure where she was going.

ABOUT THE AUTHOR

Since graduating from West Point, Stephannie Tallent has served in the Army as a Military Intelligence officer during Desert Storm, gotten a Zoology degree, went to vet school, worked as a small animal veterinarian, and designed and published knitting patterns and books.

Throughout all that she's always wanted to be a writer, and she's finally put all her type A, soft-spoken, invisible middle-aged woman focus on that goal, writing everything from fantasy to science fiction, mysteries and romance.

She has sold stories to **Pulphouse Magazine** and the **WMG Holiday Spectacular**.

www.stephannietallent.com

Sign up for my newsletter!
https://www.stephannietallent.com/subscribe/

ALSO BY STEPHANNIE TALLENT

Short Story Collections

Gates of Wonder

The Chronicles of Dinah Lee Wright Vol 1

The Chronicles of Dinah Lee Wright Vol 2

Gratitude of the Ocean: Jolene Tomberlin Series

The Serpent in the Shallows: Jolene Tomberlin Series

The Monkey's Journal

The Kaleidoscope Jaguars of the Jungles of Mexicatl

The Mermaid of Ellis Prime

One Plus One Equals More (mystery/crime)

A Snowman Made of Sand (romance)